FArTHER
Grahame Baker-Smith

For my father, Barry Hector Baker (1927–99) and my father-in-law,
Ronald Joseph Alfred Smith (1929–2009) – G.B.S.

A TEMPLAR BOOK

First published in the UK in 2010 by Templar Books,
This softback edition published in 2011 by Templar Books,
an imprint of Bonnier Books UK,
The Plaza, 535 Kings Road, London, SW10 0SZ
www.templarco.co.uk
www.bonnierbooks.co.uk

10 9 8

ISBN 978-1-84877-133-8

Designed by Mike Jolley
Edited by Libby Hamilton

Printed in China

Acknowledgements

I would like to thank my wife Linda for her inspiration, sheer
gorgeousness and for rescuing some key spreads by the careful
application of her artistic eye. Also my children – Albie, Flossie
and Lillie – whose energy and enthusiasm remains undiminished
despite my pleas for quiet and who will, I'm sure, fly to and walk
upon those distant peaks that I only glimpse through the mist.
    I also want to thank the wonderful people at Templar for
helping me to achieve my dream. Their bold approach
to publishing has made them a veritable force of nature!
I particularly want to thank Mike Jolley, who makes it all look
so good with his boundless patience and creativity.
    And also to the hound Rodney Seal for his consummate
professionalism in front of camera and his truly magnificent ears!
And to his owners – Jeremy, Ashley, Anna and Lizzie – thank you
for giving him the time off from whatever it is that he normally
does! Without him this book would definitely have fewer dogs in it.

FArTHER

Grahame Baker-Smith

templar
books

POPPIES LINED THE PATH TO MY FATHER'S HOUSE.
IT WAS MADE OF STONE AND SLATE
AND FASTENED DEEP INTO THE CLIFF.
IT WAS SAFE AND ROOTED IN THE ROCK.
BUT INSIDE MY FATHER DREAMED OF AIR AND FLIGHT.

DAY AND NIGHT, HE SEWED AND STITCHED,
AND SAWED AND HAMMERED,
AND TRIMMED THE FEATHERS
OF A THOUSAND
HOPEFUL
WINGS.

BUT SOMETIMES, THERE WAS SILENCE.

MY FATHER WOULD APPEAR AND STARE AT THE OCEAN
WITH TIRED, DISTANT EYES.

I WOULD SIT
ON HIS LAP UNTIL
HE REMEMBERED ME.

THEN, LIKE A GREAT WIND,
HE WOULD SCOOP ME UP
AND RUN OUTSIDE...

ALONG THE OLD CLIFF PATHS...   OVER THE ROCKS...

ONTO THE BEACH.

WE WOULD FISH AND SWIM AND PLAY CRICKET.
HE WOULD TEACH ME THE NAMES OF ALL THE BIRDS.

WE WOULD BE TOGETHER...
UNTIL THE **DREAM OF FLYING** RETURNED.

SUCH A BUSY,

BOSSY DREAM
THAT WOULD NOT LEAVE HIM ALONE,
OR GIVE HIM TIME TO PLAY, OR SLEEP,
OR THINK OF OTHER THINGS.

OR EVEN HAVE THE GRACE TO COME TRUE.
FOR MY FATHER, AFTER ALL, NEVER FLEW.
THOUGH HE MADE SO MANY BEAUTIFUL THINGS...

AND SO
MANY
LOVELY
WINGS...

NOTHING HE DID COULD CLAIM THE SKY.

BUT THEN ANOTHER CALL CLAIMED HIM.

I WILL ALWAYS REMEMBER THE DAY HE LEFT —
THE CLOTHES THEY GAVE HIM, KHAKI AGAINST
THE SCARLET POPPIES.

MANY YEARS PASSED

AND MY FATHER'S DREAM

WAITED UNTIL I WAS ALMOST GROWN.

AND THEN ONE DAY
IT SPOKE TO ME.

I TOOK UP
THE OLD WINGS,
MADE A FEW SIMPLE ADJUSTMENTS...

AND FLEW.

IN THE VAST BLUE SKY, I FELT MY FATHER WITH ME.

I SOON BECAME A COMMON AND EVERYDAY SIGHT AROUND THESE PARTS,

MAKING MYSELF USEFUL AND HELPING WHEREVER I COULD.

AND NOW I HAVE MY OWN SON...

WHAT WILL HE DO,
I WONDER,
IF MY FATHER'S DREAM
SHOULD VISIT HIM?